Level 2 is ideal for children who have received some reading instruction... simple sentences with help...

Special features:

Frequent repetition of main story words and phrases

Short, simple sentences

One day, Town Mouse went to see Country Mouse.

"What a funny house!" said Town Mouse. "What funny food! What a funny bed!"

8

9

Large, clear type

"What a funny house," said Country Mouse. "What funny food! What a funny bed!"

The two mice went for a walk.

Careful match between story and pictures

20

21

Educational Consultant: Geraldine Taylor
Book Banding Consultant: Kate Ruttle

A catalogue record for this book is available from the British Library

Published by Ladybird Books Ltd
80 Strand, London, WC2R 0RL
A Penguin Company

001

© LADYBIRD BOOKS LTD MMX. This edition MMXIII
Ladybird, Read It Yourself and the Ladybird Logo are registered or
unregistered trademarks of Ladybird Books Limited.

ISBN: 978-0-72327-282-3

Printed in China

Town Mouse and Country Mouse

Illustrated by Alexandra Steele-Morgan

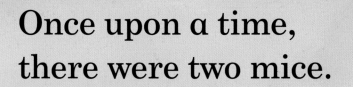

Once upon a time,
there were two mice.

Country Mouse lived
in the country.

Town Mouse lived
in the town.

7

One day, Town Mouse
went to see Country Mouse.

"What a funny house!"
said Town Mouse. "What
funny food! What a
funny bed!"

9

The two mice went
for a walk.

Suddenly, they heard
a noise:

Moo!

"What's that?"
said Town Mouse.

"It's only a cow,"
said Country Mouse.

But Town Mouse
was very frightened.

Then they heard
another noise:

Hiss!

"What's that?"
said Town Mouse.

"It's only a goose,"
said Country Mouse.

But Town Mouse
was very frightened.

Then they heard
another noise:

Whoo!

"What's that?"
said Town Mouse.

"It's the owl,"
said Country Mouse.
"Run as fast as you can!"

"I don't like it in
the country,"
said Town Mouse.
"Come with me
back to the town."

So off they went.

Town

"What a funny house,"
said Country Mouse.
"What funny food!
What a funny bed!"

The two mice went
for a walk.

Suddenly, they
heard a noise:

Parp! Parp!

"What's that?"
said Country Mouse.

"It's only a car,"
said Town Mouse.

But Country Mouse
was very frightened.

Then they heard
another noise:

Nee-naw!

"What's that?"
said Country Mouse.

"It's only a fire engine,"
said Town Mouse.

But Country Mouse
was very frightened.

25

Then they heard
another noise:

Miaow!

"What's that?"
said Country Mouse.

"It's the cat!"
said Town Mouse.
"Run as fast as you can!"

27

And Country Mouse ran
very fast – all the way
back to the country.

Country

How much do you remember about the story of Town Mouse and Country Mouse? Answer these questions and find out!

- ## What makes the noise "Hiss!"?

- ## What makes the noise "Parp! Parp!"?

- ## What do the mice run away from in the country?

- ## What do the mice run away from in the town?

Look at the pictures and match them to the story words.

Country Mouse

Town Mouse

goose

owl

fire engine

Read it yourself with Ladybird

Tick the books you've read!

For beginner readers who can read short, simple sentences with help. **Level 2**

 Beauty and the Beast ☐
 Chicken Licken ☐

 Little Red Riding Hood ☐
 Nature Trail ☐
 Sports Day ☐
 Pirate School ☐
 Rumpelstiltskin ☐
 Sleeping Beauty ☐
 The Gingerbread Man ☐

 Sly Fox and Red Hen ☐
 The Tale of Jemima Puddle-Duck ☐
 The Three Little Pigs ☐
 Why Lion Roarrrs! ☐
 Topsy and Tim The Big Race ☐
 Town Mouse and Country Mouse ☐
 Dom's Dragon ☐

For more confident readers who can read simple stories with help. **Level 3**

 YOU won't like this present as much as I DO! ☐
 The Elves and the Shoemaker ☐

 Hansel and Gretel ☐
 Harry and the Bucketful of Dinosaurs ☐
 Jack and the Beanstalk ☐
 Furi on Music Island ☐
 Poppet Stows Away ☐
 Rapunzel ☐
 The Red Knight ☐